Happy Birthday,
Alexander!

To my little birthday bunny
on his special day.
Love, Gran Gran

Battle Bunny

SIMON & SCHUSTER BOOKS FOR YOUNG READERS
An imprint of Simon & Schuster Children's Publishing Division
1230 Avenue of the Americas, New York, New York 10020
For information about special discounts for bulk purchases, please contact Simon & Schuster Special
Sales at 1-866-506-1949 or business@simonandschuster.com.
The Simon & Schuster Speakers Bureau can bring authors to your live event. For more information
or to book an event, contact the Simon & Schuster Speakers Bureau at 1-866-248-3049 or visit our
website at www.simonspeakers.com.
Book design by Dan Potash

The text for this book is set in Bitstream Cooper BT.
The illustrations for this book are rendered in oils and pencil.
Manufactured in China
0713 SCP
10 9 8 7 6 5 4 3 2 1

blast off!

Library of Congress Cataloging-in-Publication Data
Barnett, Mac.
Battle Bunny / by Jon Scieszka and Mac Barnett and Alex ; pictures by Matthew Myers but mostly
Alex. — 1st ed.
p. cm.
Summary: Alex, whose birthday it is, hijacks a story about Birthday Bunny on his special day and turns
it into a battle between a supervillain and his enemies in the forest—who, in the original story, are
simply planning a surprise party.
ISBN 978-1-4424-4673-1 (hardcover) — ISBN 978-1-4424-4674-8 (eBook)
[1. Birthdays—Fiction. 2. Rabbits—Fiction. 3. Supervillains—Fiction. 4. Forest animals—Fiction.
5. Parties—Fiction. 6. Humorous stories.] I. Scieszka, Jon. II. Myers, Matthew, ill. III. Title.
PZ7.B26615Att 2013
[E]—dc23
2012025515

Birthday Bunny

by Jon Scieszka and Mac Barnett

Pictures by Matthew Myers

Simon & Schuster Books for Young Readers

New York   London   Toronto   Sydney   New Delhi

Bunny woke up from a night of pleasant dreams. *Today is a very special day,* he thought.

Today is my birthday. Today, I am not just a bunny.

I am the ~~Birthday~~ **aTTle** Bunny!

attle
Birthday Bunny made himself his favorite

brdin   greasy guts.
breakfast: ~~carrot~~ juice and a bowl of ~~Carrot Crispies.~~

"My birthday is the most special day of the year

                                owers over
because I get super birthday ~~presents from~~ all my enemies.

              put my Evil Plan into action.
~~friends.~~ ~~And I get to do whatever I want.~~ I wonder

              try and stop me?
who will be the first to ~~give me a present?~~"

Birthday Bunny started on his ~~path~~ ^Evil Plan,^ chopping through the trees.

On the way, ~~Birthday~~ ^{attle} Bunny met Crow.

"~~Hello~~ ^{alt}, Bunny!" said Crow. "Today is ~~a special~~ ^{your unlucky} day!"

"That is so ~~true~~ ^{false}!" said ~~Birthday~~ ^{attle} Bunny. Because today I am going to whomp on you, birdbrain, and pluck you like a sick chicken!

Mr. president, Battle Bunny is up to something no good!

Thanks, Alex. I will put my best agents on it.

Crow swooped down. "I am saving ~~shiny pebbles~~ the forest from ~~your~~ Evil Plan ~~for my Sparkly Nest. And I~~ ~~have just~~ will ~~finished my~~ you off with ~~collection.~~ my megatron bombs!

"Oh," said Birthday Bunny. "I will be on my way."

Battle Bunny hopped ~~sadly past Crow~~ into the stratosphere.

Aicee "Bye, Bunny," said Crow, and flew off into the sky.

attle

Battle Bunny kept chopping through the woods

until he saw Badger.

Freeze

"Greetings, Bunny," said Badger. "Why are you Stop

chopping so madly! Today is a special day."

you face El Tejon,

the greatest wrestler!?!

evil gas

Stop!

"Yes, it is!" said Bunny.

Badger motioned with his paw. "Today I found a perfect spot for my burrow, next to a big, shady tree."

"Oh," said Birthday Bunny. "I suppose that is special."

caramba

"Good-bye, Bunny!" said Badger. He went back to digging.

down for the count.

attle
~~Birthday~~ Bunny hopped and hopped until he saw

Sgt. Squirrel, of the Robot Police Force.
in the name of the LAW!

"Stop ~~for a moment. I have a surprise,~~" said

Judgment
Sgt. Squirrel. "Today is ~~a special~~ day!"

attle
"Yes, it is!" said the ~~Birthday~~ Bunny. Judgment day for you!!

Sgt. Squirrel smiled. "Today is a special day because I

robot killer bees
have ~~stored so many nuts~~ in my tree and now I am

to sting your butt and save the
~~ready for the winter.~~ forest!!

Birthday Bunny frowned.

"Yes, that is special."

"You should plan to save too, Bunny!" said Squirrel, scampering up her tree.

B~~irthday~~ attle Bunny felt so very ~~sad~~ strong. "No one can stop ~~re~~me~~mbers it's~~ on my special day. And now my Plan ~~day~~ is almost done."!

B~~irthday~~ attle Bunny sat on ~~a stump.~~ his throne.

This is getting bad, mr. president. You really need my help.
air force one
Uh, we don't need any kid's help. I am calling in the Kenji Fighting Force.

haolin ninja
Soon Bear and Turtle came walking down the path

together.

u have dishonored the forest,
"Yoo-hoo! Yoo-hoo! Over here, Bunny!" they said.

sent by the president to eliminate
"We were looking all over the forest to find you."

attle
"You were?" said the Birthday Bunny.

you will taste our 1,108 fighting
"Yes. For today is a special day!"

I know 1104!
attle styles.
"Yes, it is special!" said the Birthday Bunny.

The ~~Birthday~~ *attle* Bunny felt like ~~crying again.~~ *the best bad guy ever*

~~Birthday~~ *attle* Bunny went to his ~~Special Thinking~~ *Evil Plan*
Place—a ~~big gray rock~~ *launchpad* in the Great Meadow.

Everybody needs a~~Special Thinking~~ *n Evil Plan* Place where
they can ~~think~~ *launch* their ~~best thoughts.~~ *Evil Plans.* Where is your
~~Special Thinking~~ *Evil Plan* Place?

~~Birthday~~ *attle* Bunny thought, *I just ~~want everyone to~~ need a few more pieces
~~remember my birthday.~~ for Plan.*

~~He thought about his friends, the other animals in~~ *sliced up Mount Everest. He knocked*
~~over the forest, and how they had forgotten his special day.~~ *Eiffel Tower. He took the arm off the Statue of Liberty.*

Maybe I will just ~~never have another birthday~~ drain the power from the sun
~~again,~~ thought ~~Birthday~~ *attle* Bunny.

Liberty

attle   heard
~~Birthday~~ Bunny ~~had been thinking so hard he~~

~~didn't hear~~ a rustling in the bushes behind him.

"SURPRISE!" ~~shouted Battle Bunny.~~ I have built a monster rocket and put mind control helmets on all my enemies.

"Today is a special day," said all the forest ~~animals~~ zombies at once.

"It is~~?~~!" said the ~~Birthday~~ Battle Bunny. HA HA HA HA

"Yes. BECAUSE IT IS YOUR BIRTHDAY! AND THIS IS DOOMS

MY YOUR SPECIAL ~~SURPRISE BIRTHDAY PARTY~~ EVIL DOOMS BATTLE THAT ~~WE~~ I

HAVE BEEN PLANNING ALL ALONG."

"Oh!" said the ~~Birthday~~ Battle Bunny. "All my friends

are ~~wonderful~~ eaks attack!"

obeyed
Crow gave Bunny his shiniest stone.

obeyed
Badger gave Bunny a drum made from a log.

obeyed
Squirrel gave Bunny a clock made out of nuts.

And Bear and Turtle ~~gave~~ obeyed Bunny ~~a necktie made from~~ most of all. ~~his handkerchief.~~

The animals all ate carrot cake and laughed and danced, and laughed and danced some more.

Then Bunny stood in the middle of the clearing. "I ~~surrender!~~

~~have a special birthday speech to make,~~" he said.

Alex, You have ~~surprised~~ defeat me with the greatest birthday

~~present.~~ owers.

great job, agent Alex!

you are the best.
"Now I know that ~~every day is special if it's a day~~

And you have the best ~~spent with your~~ friends."

"Hooray!" shouted the animals in the forest, and the president.

It was a special day indeed.